WHEN SHLEMIEL WENT TO WARSAW

Isaac Bashevis Singer

When Shlemiel Went to Warsaw & Other Stories

PICTURES BY MARGOT ZEMACH

Translated by the author and Elizabeth Shub

A Sunburst Book

Farrar, Straus and Giroux

Text copyright © 1968 by Isaac Bashevis Singer
Pictures copyright © 1968 by Margot Zemach
Library of Congress catalog card number: 68-30932
Published in Canada by HarperCollinsCanadaLtd
Printed in the United States of America
First edition, 1968
Sunburst edition, 1986
Fifth printing, 1994

Some of these stories my mother told me. These are folk tales she heard from her mother and grandmother. I have retold them in my own fashion, totally re-creating them in plot, detail and perspective. Other stories in this collection are nothing but my own imagination; these include "Tsirtsur and Peziza," "Rabbi Leib and the Witch Cunegunde," and "Menaseh's Dream." All the stories are products of a way of life rich in fantasy and make-believe.

In my writing there is no basic difference between tales for adults and for young people. The same spirit, the same interest in the supernatural is in all of them. I even mention the same villages and towns. In our time, when literature is losing its address and the telling of stories is becoming a forgotten art, children are the best readers.

I dedicate this volume to the memory of my father and mother—great and enthusiastic storytellers, persons of deep faith and love of man, especially of all Shlemiels, old and young.

I.B.S.

Shrewd Todie &
Lyzer the Miser

In a village somewhere in the Ukraine there lived a poor man called Todie. Todie had a wife, Shaindel, and seven children, but he could never earn enough to feed them properly. He tried many trades and failed in all of them. It was said of Todie that if he decided to deal in candles the sun would never set. He was nicknamed Shrewd Todie because whenever he managed to make some money, it was always by trickery.

This winter was an especially cold one. The snowfall was heavy and Todie had no money to buy wood for the stove. His seven children stayed in bed all day to keep warm. When the frost burns outside, hunger is stronger than ever, but Shaindel's larder was empty. She reproached Todie bitterly, wailing, "If you can't feed your wife and children, I will go to the rabbi and get a divorce."

"And what will you do with it, eat it?" Todie retorted.

In the same village there lived a rich man called Lyzer. Because of his stinginess he was known as Lyzer the Miser. He permitted his wife to bake bread only once in four weeks because he had discovered that fresh bread is eaten up more quickly than stale.

Todie had more than once gone to Lyzer for a loan of a few gulden, but Lyzer had always replied: "I sleep better when the money lies in my strongbox rather than in your pocket."

Lyzer had a goat, but he never fed her. The goat had learned to visit the houses of the neighbors, who pitied her and gave her potato peelings. Sometimes, when there were not enough peelings, she would gnaw on the old straw of the thatched roofs. She also had a liking for tree bark. Nevertheless, each year the goat gave birth to a kid. Lyzer milked her but, miser that he was, did not drink the milk himself. Instead he sold it to others.

Todie decided that he would take revenge on Lyzer

and at the same time make some much-needed money for himself.

One day, as Lyzer was sitting on a box eating borscht and dry bread (he used his chairs only on holidays so that the upholstery would not wear out), the door opened and Todie came in.

"Reb Lyzer," he said, "I would like to ask you a favor. My oldest daughter, Basha, is already fifteen and she's about to become engaged. A young man is coming from Janev to look her over. My cutlery is tin, and my wife is ashamed to ask the young man to eat soup with a tin spoon. Would you lend me one of your silver spoons? I give you my holy word that I will return it to you tomorrow."

Lyzer knew that Todie would not dare to break a holy oath and he lent him the spoon.

No young man came to see Basha that evening. As usual, the girl walked around barefoot and in rags, and the silver spoon lay hidden under Todie's shirt. In the early years of his marriage Todie had possessed a set of silver tableware himself. He had, however, long since sold it all, with the exception of three silver teaspoons that were used only on Passover.

The following day, as Lyzer, his feet bare (in order to save his shoes), sat on his box eating borscht and dry bread, Todie returned.

"Here is the spoon I borrowed yesterday," he said, placing it on the table together with one of his own teaspoons.

"What is the teaspoon for?" Lyzer asked.

And Todie said: "Your tablespoon gave birth to a teaspoon. It is her child. Since I am an honest man, I'm returning both mother and child to you."

Lyzer looked at Todie in astonishment. He had never heard of a silver spoon giving birth to another. Nevertheless, his greed overcame his doubt and he happily accepted both spoons. Such an unexpected piece of good fortune! He was overjoyed that he had loaned Todie the spoon.

A few days later, as Lyzer (without his coat, to save it) was again sitting on his box eating borscht with dry bread, the door opened and Todie appeared.

"The young man from Janev did not please Basha because he had donkey ears, but this evening another young man is coming to look her over. Shaindel is cooking soup for him, but she's ashamed to serve him with a tin spoon. Would you lend me . . ."

Even before Todie could finish the sentence, Lyzer interrupted. "You want to borrow a silver spoon? Take it with pleasure."

The following day Todie once more returned the spoon and with it one of his own silver teaspoons. He again

explained that during the night the large spoon had given birth to a small one and in all good conscience he was bringing back the mother and newborn baby. As for the young man who had come to look Basha over, she hadn't liked him either, because his nose was so long that it reached to his chin. Needless to say that Lyzer the Miser was overjoyed.

Exactly the same thing happened a third time. Todie related that this time his daughter had rejected her suitor because he stammered. He also reported that Lyzer's silver spoon had again given birth to a baby spoon.

"Does it ever happen that a spoon has twins?" Lyzer inquired.

Todie thought it over for a moment. "Why not? I've even heard of a case where a spoon had triplets."

Almost a week passed by and Todie did not go to see Lyzer. But on Friday morning, as Lyzer (in his under-drawers to save his pants) sat on his box eating borscht and dry bread, Todie came in and said, "Good day to you, Reb Lyzer."

"A good morning and many more to you," Lyzer replied in his friendliest manner. "What good fortune brings you here? Did you perhaps come to borrow a silver spoon? If so, help yourself."

"Today I have a very special favor to ask. This evening a young man from the big city of Lublin is coming to look Basha over. He is the son of a rich man and I'm told he is clever and handsome as well. Not only do I need a silver spoon, but since he will remain with us over the Sabbath I need a pair of silver candlesticks, because mine are brass and my wife is ashamed to place them on the Sabbath table. Would you lend me your candlesticks? Immediately after the Sabbath, I will return them to you."

Silver candlesticks are of great value and Lyzer the Miser hesitated, but only for a moment.

Remembering his good fortune with the spoons, he said: "I have eight silver candlesticks in my house. Take them all. I know you will return them to me just as you say. And if it should happen that any of them give birth, I have no doubt that you will be as honest as you have been in the past."

"Certainly," Todie said. "Let's hope for the best."

The silver spoon, Todie hid beneath his shirt as usual. But taking the candlesticks, he went directly to a merchant, sold them for a considerable sum, and brought the money to Shaindel. When Shaindel saw so much money, she demanded to know where he had gotten such a treasure.

"When I went out, a cow flew over our roof and dropped a dozen silver eggs," Todie replied. "I sold them and here is the money."

"I have never heard of a cow flying over a roof and laying silver eggs," Shaindel said doubtingly.

"There is always a first time," Todie answered. "If you don't want the money, give it back to me."

"There'll be no talk about giving it back," Shaindel said. She knew that her husband was full of cunning and tricks—but when the children are hungry and the larder is empty, it is better not to ask too many questions. Shaindel went to the marketplace and bought meat, fish, white flour, and even some nuts and raisins for a pudding. And since a lot of money still remained, she bought shoes and clothes for the children.

It was a very gay Sabbath in Todie's house. The boys sang and the girls danced. When the children asked their father where he had gotten the money, he replied: "It is forbidden to mention money during the Sabbath."

Sunday, as Lyzer (barefoot and almost naked to save his clothes) sat on his box finishing up a dry crust of bread with borscht, Todie arrived and, handing him his silver spoon, said: "It's too bad. This time your spoon did not give birth to a baby."

"What about the candlesticks?" Lyzer inquired anxiously.

Todie sighed deeply. "The candlesticks died."

Lyzer got up from his box so hastily that he over-turned his plate of borscht.

"You fool! How can candlesticks die?" he screamed.

"If spoons can give birth, candlesticks can die."

Lyzer raised a great hue and cry and had Todie called before the rabbi. When the rabbi heard both sides of the story, he burst out laughing. "It serves you right," he said to Lyzer. "If you hadn't chosen to believe that spoons give birth, now you would not be forced to believe that your candlesticks died."

"But it's all nonsense," Lyzer objected.

"Did you not expect the candlesticks to give birth to other candlesticks?" the rabbi said admonishingly. "If you accept nonsense when it brings you profit, you must also accept nonsense when it brings you loss." And he dismissed the case.

The following day, when Lyzer the Miser's wife brought him his borscht and dry bread, Lyzer said to her, "I will eat only the bread. Borscht is too expensive a food, even without sour cream."

The story of the silver spoons that gave birth and the candlesticks that died spread quickly through the town. All the people enjoyed Todie's victory and Lyzer the Miser's defeat. The shoemaker's and tailor's apprentices, as was their custom whenever there was an important happening, made up a song about it:

> *Lyzer, put your grief aside.*
> *What if your candlesticks have died?*

> *You're the richest man on earth*
> *With silver spoons that can give birth*
> *And silver eggs as living proof*
> *Of flying cows above your roof.*
> *Don't sit there eating crusts of bread—*
> *To silver grandsons look ahead.*

However, time passed and Lyzer's silver spoons never gave birth again.

Tsirtsur & Peziza

In a dark space between the stove and the wall, where the housewife stored her brooms, mops, and baking paddles, there lived an orphan imp called Peziza. She had only one friend in the world, Tsirtsur, a cricket. He too made his home behind the stove in a crevice between two bricks. An imp doesn't have to eat at all, but how Tsirtsur managed to survive is a riddle. Perhaps just the smell of fresh bread baking, a speck of flour that a house breeze swept back there, a drop of moisture in the air were enough for him. In any case, Tsirtsur never complained to Peziza about the lack of food. He dozed all day long. When evening came, he was wide awake and began chirping stories that often continued through the night.

Peziza had never known her father, Lantuch the Imp. Her mother, Pashtida, who came from a wealthy family, had fallen in love with Lantuch. She had often told Peziza about the world that existed beyond the stove and about their relatives, the devils, gnomes, and hobgoblins, each with his own tricks and deviltries. Even so, if one has spent one's entire life behind a stove, one knows little of what is going on in the world, and Peziza had a strong curiosity, a trait no doubt inherited from her parents. While Tsirtsur chirped out his endless tales, Peziza dreamed of impish adventures.

Sometimes Peziza would ask Tsirtsur to tell her how it was outside and he would reply: "My mother said there's only trouble. Cold winds blow, cruel creatures devour each other."

"Nevertheless," Peziza would say thoughtfully, "I'd like to have a look myself at what the devils out there are doing."

And that is exactly what Fate had in mind.

One day there was a loud pounding and hammering. The stove shook, bricks fell. Peziza flew up and down in fright. The houseowners had decided to rebuild the stove. The racket continued all day long and both creatures huddled together until evening. When a piece of wall fell away, Tsirtsur cried, "If we don't get out of here, we'll be killed." There was a break which reached to the outside. They crept through it and found themselves in the back yard of the house. They stood on grass among shrubs and trees. It was the first time Peziza and Tsirtsur had breathed fresh air.

How beautiful the outside was! A huge sky, a moon, stars. Dew was forming. There was the whirring of myriads of crickets. They sounded just like Tsirtsur.

"I will dig myself a hole," Tsirtsur said, "because when the sun rises I must not stay in the open."

"My mother too warned me against the sun," Peziza agreed. "But a hole in the earth is not a proper hiding place for me. There is a hollow in that tree. I will spend the day there."

"The most important thing is that we don't lose each other," Tsirtsur declared. "I'll dig my hole near the roots of your tree."

Tsirtsur immediately began digging. He spoke to Peziza as he worked. "As long as it is summer, the outdoors is not so dangerous. But winter is a bitter time for crickets. It gets cold and something called snow covers the ground. Few crickets survive in such weather."

"Do you mind if I take a look around while you're busy?" Peziza asked.

"You may get lost."

"I won't fly far. I'll recognize this tree. It is taller than the others."

Tsirtsur urged Peziza not to wander away. But curious Peziza was not yet ready to settle down in her hollow. Her desire to see all the new things around her was too strong. She flew off and came to rest on a roof. "I never knew I could fly so well," she thought. Suddenly she heard someone calling to her. She looked in the direction of the voice and saw an imp perched on a weather vane. Although the only other imp Peziza had ever seen was her mother, she knew at once that this imp was a young man. He had two pairs of wings and his horns were transparent. "What is your name?" he asked.

Peziza was so surprised that for a moment she remained speechless. Then she said, "Peziza."

"Peziza? My name is Paziz."

"Is that true or are you joking?"

"Why should I joke? That is my name. Maybe we're related. Let's fly."

Paziz jumped down from the weather vane and somersaulted over the roof to Peziza. He took off and she flew after him, amazed that she was not afraid. The night was full of shadowy creatures. Imps, shades, goblins. One danced on a chimney, another slid down a drainpipe, a third whirled around using a weather vane as a carousel, a fourth clambered up a lamppost. Paziz flew so quickly that it made Peziza dizzy, but she managed to keep up with him. They passed over fields, forests, rivers, lakes, hamlets, and towns. As they flew along, Paziz entertained Peziza with stories of ruined castles, broken windmills, and forsaken houses. How large the world was! How strange the night! How endless the roads! Peziza could have flown on forever, but she knew that when the cock crows and the sun rises, an imp must hide. She also missed Tsirtsur.

"Where are we?" she asked. "I hope I will recognize my tree."

"There is no lack of trees here," Paziz remarked.

"Yes, but my friend Tsirtsur the cricket is waiting for me."

"What kind of a friendship is that? An imp and a cricket?"

"We've always been together. I could never live without him," Peziza replied.

"Very well then. I will bring you back to where we started from."

They had been flying swiftly, but homeward bound they traveled even more quickly than before. In her dreams Peziza had never imagined an imp as clever and brave as Paziz was. He had not spent his life, as she had, in a dark space between a stove and a wall. Each day he found a different resting place. At night he wandered wherever he pleased. He made many friends.

At last the roof where Paziz and Peziza had met came into view and Peziza recognized her tree nearby. To her amazement, when they landed she saw that Tsirtsur was not alone. There was another cricket with him. Tsirtsur too had found a friend and the new cricket was helping him dig his home.

"Where have you been?" Tsirtsur called when he saw Peziza. "I was afraid you were lost."

"I never would have found my way back had it not been for Paziz," she replied and introduced the imp to Tsirtsur.

Tsirtsur cricked politely: "As you see, I too have found a friend. Her name is Grillida."

Fate always has surprises up its sleeve. When Peziza and Tsirtsur were forced to leave their home behind the stove, they were sure their end was near. But the powers that be had their own plans. Instead of misfortune, Peziza found Paziz and Tsirtsur, Grillida. The couples soon became so attached to each other that they were inseparable and before long were married according to the customs of imps and crickets.

As long as summer lasted, they all enjoyed the outdoors. Paziz and Peziza spent their nights flying about and

traveled as far as the big city of Lublin. Tsirtsur and Grillida amused themselves by telling each other stories. When day came, the crickets rested in the nest they had dug and the imps slept in their tree hollow.

Little by little the nights began to get cool. A mist rose from the river. The frogs croaked less frequently. One seldom heard the whirring of crickets. Tsirtsur and Grillida kept close together for warmth. Sometimes it rained, lightninged, and thundered at night. Paziz and Peziza did not suffer from the cold, but they, too, had their troubles. First, they felt sorry for their friends, the crickets. Second, the tree in which they lived stood not far from the synagogue and every day they were disturbed by the blowing of the ram's horn. It is known that imps are afraid of the sound of a ram's horn. Whenever Peziza heard the horn's blast, she began to tremble and cry.

One evening Peziza noticed that the chimney leading to the stove behind which she and Tsirtsur used to live had smoke coming out of it. It had been rebuilt and was again in use. All four friends took counsel and decided to try to get behind the stove for the winter. Peziza and Paziz would have no difficulty getting there. They could fly into the house through an open window or through the chimney when the stove was cold. But for Tsirtsur and Grillida it would be a long and difficult journey. However, with the imps helping the crickets along, they all made their way to the old space between the stove and the wall.

The days became shorter, the nights longer. Outdoors it rained and snowed. The frosts came, but behind the stove it was dark, warm, and smelled of bread, cakes, and Sabbath pudding. The owners often toasted noodles and baked apples. In the kitchen, the housewife and her daughters plucked chickens and told stories about ghosts, hobgoblins, and imps. After having spent so much time listening to the people of the house, Peziza and Tsirtsur had learned to understand the language of humans. They had long since discovered that like crickets and imps, humans too dream of love and happiness.

Tsirtsur and Grillida never again left their nest, but Paziz and Peziza would often go out through the chimney to air their wings and revel in the adventures of the netherworld. Each time they returned they brought back new stories for the stay-at-homes. Some were gay and mischievous, others devilish and frightening, but all delighted the crickets and gave Tsirtsur much to chirp about with Grillida in the long winter nights.

Rabbi Leib &
the Witch Cunegunde

Rabbi Leib, the son of Sarah, and the witch Cunegunde were both miracle workers. The difference between them was that Rabbi Leib performed his wonders with the aid of divine power and Cunegunde used the power of the devil. Cunegunde had a son, the famous brigand Bolvan who robbed merchants on the roads. He had collected a fortune in stolen goods, which he hoarded in a cave. Although Bolvan did the actual hijacking, it was Cunegunde who made all the plans. By her witchcraft she was able to make invisible the entrance to the cave where their loot was kept, so that the police could never find it. At sixty, Cunegunde still had pitch-black hair and a smooth, fresh skin. It was said that she possessed a potion that kept her looking young.

For years Rabbi Leib and Cunegunde waged silent warfare. Whenever Rabbi Leib gave a merchant an amulet to guard him against evil, Bolvan could neither rob nor harm him. This resulted in many losses for the brigand. Cunegunde tried to outwit Rabbi Leib, but his prayers usually proved stronger than her witchcraft.

Rabbi Leib was so often the winner that finally Cunegunde could not help admiring him. And from admiration to love is but one step. However, Cunegunde could only love as a witch does. Here is the letter she wrote to Rabbi Leib:

"You, Leib, are the strongest man on earth and I, Cunegunde, am the strongest woman. If we got married, we could rule the world. We could rob the greatest banks, empty the richest mints, and the mightiest rulers would tremble before us."

And Rabbi Leib's reply:

"I don't want to rob banks or empty mints. I want to serve God and not the devil. I'd rather live with a snake than with you."

When Cunegunde received Rabbi Leib's letter, her love for him became mixed with hatred. She vowed she would force him to marry her and then revenge herself on him. She wrote to him again:

"You can't escape. You will fall into my clutches. You will marry me whether you like it or not, and you will have the same bitter end as my five husbands before you." It was known that Cunegunde, five times a widow, had in each case destroyed her husband.

Rabbi Leib and Cunegunde both lived in the same huge forest. She had a luxurious underground house with a secret entrance through the hollow of a tree. He owned a small hut by a stream in which he immersed himself each morning before prayers. He liked to pray among the trees. From time to time, he went to the village nearby to purchase food. Rabbi Leib ate neither meat nor fish, nor anything else that came from a living creature. He bought his scant provisions and always laid in a large supply of seeds for the birds of the forest. Every day hundreds of them came to feed in the clearing in front of his hut. As he prayed, the birds sang and twittered and their voices lifted his spirit and strengthened his faith.

Suddenly strange things began to happen and Rabbi Leib recognized them as the work of Cunegunde. Venomous snakes appeared near his hut and attacked the birds. At night the howling of wild dogs disturbed him in his studies. One dawn as he bathed in the stream, a strange little beast not unlike a hedgehog bit into his leg with its sharp teeth. Rabbi Leib uttered a holy incantation and the beast let go. But the marks of its teeth remained behind.

Rabbi Leib bought loaves of bread fresh from the oven in the village, but when he arrived home the bread was moldy. Worms, mice, and rats invaded his hut. Rabbi Leib kept some fowl which he never slaughtered; he loved the sound of roosters crowing and chickens cackling. One night a weasel stole into his yard and killed them all.

The water of his stream, which had always been crystal clear, suddenly became muddy and began to smell.

One evening when Rabbi Leib went into the forest to pray, he noticed a man, covered with soot like a chimney sweep, on the roof of his hut. The man carried a broom as long as a sapling and a coil of thick rope. He had the wild eyes of a beast and pointed white teeth. Rabbi Leib called out to him:

> *"Creature of darkness lurking here,*
> *To the wastes of Sodom disappear."*

For a moment the demon hesitated. Then he called back: "I will not move until you listen to what I have to say."

"Who are you? What do you want?"

"My name is Hurmizah. I am the devoted servant of my mistress Cunegunde. She sent me to tell you that

she is pining away for love of you. If you do not consent to marry her, she will avenge herself on all your friends and family. She has not the power to harm you, but she can do as she pleases with the others. However, if you agree to become her husband, she will give you half her treasures, bags full of gold, diamonds, and other precious things. She will also build you a palace on Mount Seir, near Asmodeus's own castle, and have you appointed one of his seven councilors. A thousand he-demons and she-demons will do your bidding. Instead of immersing your-self in your muddy little stream, you will bathe in a pool of balsam. Naamah herself will dance for you, together with her maids. You will drink five-thousand-year-old wine from the cellars of Malkizedek." Hurmizah would have continued but Rabbi Leib intoned a holy name that he used only in cases of utmost need and Cunegunde's messenger was forced to leave. As he spread out a pair of batlike wings, he called: "Leib, think it over. I'll be back tomorrow. In the end Cunegunde's witchcraft will conquer your incantations."

He flew off, leaving behind him the smell of pitch, sulphur, and devil's dung.

That night Rabbi Leib could not sleep. He lit a candle, but the wind blew it out. From his chimney came the sound of whistling and laughter. Although he knew that Cunegunde could not harm him, he worried about his friends and relatives and about his beloved birds. He had to get rid of the witch once and for all. But how?

The following night when the demon chimney sweep appeared again on Rabbi Leib's roof, the Rabbi said to him: "Hurmizah, last night I could not sleep a wink and I thought everything over. I came to the conclusion that Cunegunde is right. She and I together would be the mightiest pair in the world. Fly to your mistress and tell her that I am prepared to marry her."

When Hurmizah heard these words, he said, "It's a good thing you've come to your senses, my lord. My mistress Cunegunde planned to destroy your house, burn down the forest, dry up the stream, and that just as a start. Nobody is mightier or more beautiful. Together you will rule over man and beast." Hurmizah departed at once to carry the good news to Cunegunde.

Cunegunde wasted no time. She dressed in her best clothes, placed a diamond tiara on her head, and adorned herself with many precious bracelets and anklets. She mounted a broom with silver whisks and flew to Rabbi Leib's hut. Behind her came her retinue: creatures with pointed noses, twisted horns, long tails, and ears reaching down to their shoulders. A giant with a nose like a ram's horn carried a fat midget as round as a pot on his back. As they traveled along, they screamed, laughed, hooted, blasphemed.

Rabbi Leib, dressed in a white robe, stepped out of his hut to greet the bridal party. The entire company landed before him. Cunegunde said: "Leib, I forgive all the injustices you committed against me. You are about to become my husband and I, your wife. As soon as we are married, the Forces of Good will lose their power and you and I, with the help of Satan, will be the lords of heaven and earth."

"Cunegunde," Rabbi Leib replied, "I tried to resist your charms, but I could not. Do with me as you wish."

"My children, put up the wedding canopy," Cunegunde ordered.

Four goblins at once brought forth a black canopy. Instead of four posts, it was supported by four snakes. From somewhere the sound of caterwauling music started up. Hurmizah gave away the bride. Another giant devil played best man to Rabbi Leib. The wedding ceremony began at dawn, just before the sun rose. Cunegunde laughed to herself. She had already figured out how to destroy Rabbi Leib. But first she had to learn his holy incantations so as to deprive him of divine power. Gloatingly she thought to herself, "With all your wisdom, Leib, you're just a fool."

One of the devils took out a black wedding ring and handed it to Rabbi Leib, who was to place it on Cunegunde's first finger. If he had done so, they would actually have become man and wife and he would have been a slave of the netherworld forever. But instead of putting the ring on her finger, Rabbi Leib said: "Cunegunde, my dear, before you become my wife, I want to give you a present."

"What kind of present?"

"A golden locket that will endow you with powers in both the upper and the nether world. Allow me to hang it around your lovely neck."

Cunegunde smiled smugly and said: "Very well, Leib. Hang your locket around my neck." And she lowered her head to help him. That was all Rabbi Leib needed. The locket held a charm blessed by the saintly Rabbi Michael of Zlotchev. Rabbi Leib placed the locket around Cunegunde's neck. Cunegunde turned to Hurmizah to show off the precious gift and to gloat over Rabbi Leib's faith in her. But suddenly she let out a terrifying scream. The locket was burning into her flesh like a fire of hell. She tried to tear it from her neck, but her hands were powerless.

Rabbi Leib had again managed to outwit the witch Cunegunde.

When the devils and hobgoblins saw that their mistress was powerless, they fled in fear. The Evil Ones are cowards at heart. Cunegunde remained alone. She fell on her knees and begged Rabbi Leib to remove the locket, promising him all the treasures in her possession. But Rabbi Leib had learned that there can be no compassion for the creatures of the netherworld. He knew what had happened in olden times to Joseph de la Rainah, the famous saint, who had captured Satan and bound him in chains. Satan had begged for some snuff and when Rabbi Joseph took pity and gave it to him, Satan turned the snuff into a fire that melted his chains and enabled him to escape.

"Cunegunde, although I now have the power to destroy you, I have decided not to kill you, but to send you to a place from which you will never be able to return." Then he incanted:

> *"Cunegunde, Keteff's daughter,*
> *To the land of Admah fly*
> *And remain there till you die."*

Admah was one of the towns destroyed in biblical times together with Sodom and Gomorrah.

In vain Cunegunde wept, implored, and made all kinds of promises. A strong wind swept her up in the air and carried her away as swiftly as an arrow flies from a bow. The locket fell from her neck and she lost her power for all time. She lived out her life in the wasteland of Admah, not far from the place where Lot's wife had been turned into a pillar of salt.

Without the protection of his mother, Cunegunde's son, Bolvan, became an ordinary thief. The police soon found the hidden cave where his loot was stored and arrested him. All the gold, precious stones, and stolen goods were returned to their rightful owners, or to their heirs. Bolvan, bound in chains, died in prison while still waiting for his trial.

From then on, Rabbi Leib lived in peace. The stream in which he immersed himself each morning was again crystal clear and the birds gathered in front of his hut to be fed. He supported the poor, cured the sick, and helped those who were possessed by evil spirits.

As long as he lived, the black host stayed away from the forest. It was only after his death that they dared to return to try their old tricks. Soon after, a new saint appeared, the famous miracle worker Reb Baruch, and the ancient war between good and evil started all over again.

The Elders of Chelm &
Genendel's Key

It was known that the village of Chelm was ruled by the head of the community council and the six Elders, all fools. The name of the head was Gronam the Ox. The Elders were Dopey Lekisch, Zeinvel Ninny, Treitel the Fool, Sender Donkey, Shmendrick Numskull, and Feyvel Thickwit. Gronam the Ox was the oldest. He had a curly white beard and a high, bulging forehead.

Since Gronam had a large house, the Elders usually met there. Every now and then Gronam's wife, Genendel, brought them refreshments—tea, cakes, and jam.

Gronam would have been a happy man except for the fact that each time the elders left, Genendel would reproach him for speaking nonsense. In her opinion her highly respected husband was a simpleton.

Once, after such a quarrel, Gronam said to his wife: "What is the sense in nagging me after the elders have gone? In the future, whenever you hear me saying something silly, come into the room and let me know. I will immediately change the subject."

"But how can I tell you you're talking nonsense in front of the Elders? If they learn you're a fool, you'll lose your job as head of the council."

"If you're so clever, find a way," Gronam replied.

Genendel thought a moment and suddenly exclaimed, "I have it."

"Well?"

"When you say something silly, I will come in and hand you the key to our strongbox. Then you'll know you've been talking like a fool."

Gronam was so delighted with his wife's idea that he clapped his hands. "Near me, you too become clever."

A few days later the Elders met in Gronam's house. The subject under discussion was the coming Pentecost, a holiday when a lot of sour cream is needed to eat with blintzes. That year there was a scarcity of sour cream. It had been a dry spring and the cows gave little milk.

The Elders pulled at their beards and rubbed their foreheads, signs that their brains were hard at work. But none of them could figure out how to get enough sour cream for the holiday.

Suddenly Gronam pounded on the table with his fist and called out: "I have it!"

"What is it?"

"Let us make a law that water is to be called sour cream and sour cream is to be called water. Since there is plenty of water in the wells of Chelm, each housewife will have a full barrel of sour cream."

"What a wonderful idea," cried Sender Donkey.

"A stroke of genius," shrieked Zeinvel Ninny.

"Only Gronam the Ox could think of something so brilliant," Dopey Lekisch proclaimed.

Treitel the Fool, Shmendrick Numskull, and Feyvel Thickwit all agreed. Feyvel Thickwit, the community scribe, took out pen and parchment and set down the new law. From that day on, water was to be called sour cream and sour cream, water.

As usual, when they had finished with community business, the Elders turned to more general subjects. Gronam said: "Last night I couldn't sleep a wink for thinking about why it is hot in the summertime. Finally the answer came to me."

"What is it?" the Elders chorused.

"Because all winter long the stoves are heated and this heat stays in Chelm and makes the summer hot."

All the Elders nodded their heads, excepting Dopey Lekisch, who asked: "Then why is it cold in the winter?"

"It's clear why," replied Gronam. "The stoves are not heated in the summer, so there is no heat left over for the winter."

The Elders were enthusiastic about Gronam's great knowledge. After such mental effort, they began to look towards the kitchen, expecting Genendel to appear with the tea, cakes, and jam.

Genendel did come in, but instead of a tray she carried a key, which she gave to her husband, saying: "Gronam, here is the key to the strongbox."

Today of all days Gronam was confident that his mouth had uttered only clever words. But there stood Genendel with the key in her hand, a sure sign that he had spoken like a fool. He grew so angry that he turned to the Elders and said: "Tell me, what foolishness have I spoken that my wife brings me the key to our strongbox?"

The Elders were perplexed at this question and Gronam explained his agreement with Genendel, that she should give him the key when he talked like an idiot. "But today, didn't I speak words of high wisdom? You be the judges."

The elders were furious with Genendel. Feyvel Thickwit

spoke out. "We are the Elders of Chelm, and we understand everything. No woman can tell us what is wise and what is silly."

They then discussed the matter and made a new law: whenever Genendel believed that her husband was talking like a fool, she was to come in and give the key to the Elders. If they agreed, they would tell Gronam the Ox to change the subject. If they did not agree, she was to bring out a double portion of tea, cakes, and jam and three blintzes for every sage.

Feyvel Thickwit immediately recorded the new law on parchment and stamped it with the seal of Chelm, which was an ox with six horns.

From that day on, Gronam could talk freely at the meetings, since Genendel was very stingy. She did not want the Elders of Chelm to gorge themselves with her beloved blintzes.

That Pentecost there was no lack of "sour cream" in Chelm, but some housewives complained that there was a lack of "water." But this was an entirely new problem, to be solved after the holiday.

Gronam the Ox became famous all over the world as the sage who—by passing a law—gave Chelm a whole river and many wells full of sour cream.

Shlemiel,
the Businessman

Shlemiel, who lived in Chelm, was not always a stay-at-home and there was a time when his wife did not sell vegetables in the marketplace. Mrs. Shlemiel's father was a man of means and when his daughter married Shlemiel, he gave her a dowry.

Shortly after the wedding, Shlemiel decided to use the dowry to go into business. He had heard that in Lublin goats could be bought cheaply and he went there to buy one. He wanted a milk goat so that he could make cheese to sell. The goat dealer offered him a goat whose large udders were filled with milk. Shlemiel paid him the five gulden he asked for the goat, tied a string around its neck, and led it back toward Chelm.

On the way home, Shlemiel stopped in the village of Piask, known for its thieves and swindlers although Shlemiel was not aware of this. He went into an inn to eat and left the goat tethered to a tree in the courtyard.

He ordered some sweet brandy, an appetizer of chopped liver with onions, a plate of chicken soup with noodles, and, as befits a successful businessman, some tea and honey cake for dessert. Before long he began to feel the effects of the brandy. He boasted to the innkeeper about the wonderful animal he had picked up in Lublin. "What a bargain I got," he announced. "A young, healthy goat, and what a great milker she promises to be."

The innkeeper, who happened to be a typical Piask swindler, owned an old billy goat that was blind in one eye and had a long white beard and a broken horn. Only the fact that it was so emaciated saved it from the butcher. After listening to Shlemiel praise his new goat, the innkeeper went into the courtyard and replaced Shlemiel's young animal with his old one. Shlemiel was so preoccupied with his business plans that he hardly looked at the goat when he untied it and so didn't notice that he was leading back to Chelm a different goat from the one he had bought.

Since it was Shlemiel's first business venture, the entire family was waiting impatiently to see the animal he was bringing back from the big city. They were all gathered in Shlemiel's house—his father-in-law, his brothers- and sisters-in-law, as well as friends and neighbors. When Shlemiel finally arrived, they ran out to the yard to greet him. Even before he opened the gate, he began to extol the virtues of his purchase—the goat's strength, its full udders.

When the old billy goat followed Shlemiel through the gate, there was consternation. His father-in-law clutched at his beard, dumfounded. His mother-in-law spread her arms in a gesture of bewilderment. The young men laughed and the young women giggled. His father-in-law was the first one to speak up: "Is this what you call a young goat? It's a half-dead billy."

At first Shlemiel protested violently, but then for the first time he took a good look at the animal he had brought home. When he saw the old billy goat, he beat his head with his fists. He was convinced that the goat dealer had cheated him, although he could not figure out when he could have managed to do so. Shlemiel was so furious that after a sleepless night he set out for Lublin to return the goat and give the dealer a piece of his mind.

On the way he again stopped in Piask, at the same inn. He told the innkeeper that he had been swindled in Lublin and that he was on his way to get the right goat or his money back. If the merchant did not give him satisfaction, he intended to call the police. The innkeeper had more than once been in trouble with the authorities. He realized that an investigation might lead to him and that was the last thing he wanted.

As Shlemiel poured out his complaints against the Lublin goat dealer, the innkeeper clicked his tongue in sympathy and said: "It's well known that the merchants of Lublin are cheaters. Be watchful or you will be swindled a second time." Soon thereafter, as Shlemiel was busy eating his lunch, the innkeeper went out into the courtyard and again exchanged the goats. When Shlemiel was ready to leave, he was so preoccupied with imagining what he would say to the dealer that he again paid little attention to the animal he was leading.

Shlemiel arrived at the goat dealer's and began to threaten and upbraid him. The astonished dealer pointed out that the goat Shlemiel was returning was indeed young and had milk-filled udders. Shlemiel took one look at the goat and was left speechless. When at last he found his tongue, he exclaimed: "All I can say is that I must have been seeing things." He apologized profusely, took the goat, and again started back to Chelm. When he reached Piask, he as usual stopped at the inn for some refreshment. He ordered chicken and dumplings and, to

celebrate the fact that he had made a good bargain after all, some sweet brandy. The innkeeper, born thief that he was, couldn't resist swindling such an easy victim. Offering Shlemiel a second brandy on the house, he went out into the yard and again exchanged the goats.

When Shlemiel left the inn, night was falling. By this time he was a bit tipsy and hardly glanced at the goat as he untied it and started for home.

When Shlemiel returned to Chelm for the second time leading an old billy goat instead of a young female, there was pandemonium. Word spread quickly and the whole town went wild. The matter was immediately brought before the Elders, who deliberated seven days and seven nights and came to the conclusion that when a nanny goat is taken from Lublin to Chelm it turns into a billy goat on the way. They therefore proclaimed a law prohibiting the import of goats from Lublin by any resident of Chelm. The old goat soon died and Shlemiel had lost one third of his wife's dowry.

Shlemiel, having failed in his business dealings with Lublin, decided to try his luck in Lemberg. He had no sooner arrived in that city and settled himself in his room at the inn than the street on which it was located was filled with the screams of people and the continuous loud blast of a trumpet. Shlemiel had slept little on his way to Lemberg and had gone to bed on his arrival. He called for a servant to ask what the commotion was all about and was told that a house across the road was on fire and that the fire wagons had arrived. Shlemiel might have gone out to look at the fire, but he was exhausted from his long journey. After being assured that there was no danger to the inn and that the fire was being extinguished, he dozed off.

On awakening, he went to the lobby and asked one of the guests how the fire had started and how long it had taken to put it out. "Was it done merely by blowing a trumpet?" he wanted to know.

The man Shlemiel addressed happened to be one of Lemberg's most cunning thieves and Shlemiel's question immediately gave him an idea. "Yes," he replied. "Here in Lemberg we have a trumpet that extinguishes fires. It has only to be blown and the fire goes out."

Shlemiel could hardly express his amazement. He had heard of the many wonders of Lemberg, but never of a fire-fighting trumpet. It immediately occurred to him what a great source of profit such a trumpet could be in a town like Chelm, where all the houses were made of wood and most of the roofs of straw.

"How much does such a trumpet cost?" Shlemiel inquired.

"Two hundred gulden," the man replied.

Two hundred gulden was a large sum of money. It amounted to almost the entire remainder of Mrs. Shlemiel's dowry. But when Shlemiel thought it over, he came to the conclusion that such a trumpet was more than worth the money. In Chelm there were many fires each year, especially in summertime. Houses and entire streets burned down. Although there were several firemen in Chelm, their equipment consisted of a single wagon drawn by an ancient nag. By the time the wagon arrived with its one barrel of water, everything had usually burned down. Shlemiel hadn't the slightest doubt that the owner of a fire-fighting trumpet could make a fortune. He told the man that he would like to buy such a trumpet and the other was more than willing to supply one. It was not long before he delivered a huge brass trumpet and a written guarantee that when blown it would extinguish all fires.

Shlemiel was overjoyed. This time he was sure he was on his way to becoming a rich man.

Back in Chelm, Shlemiel displayed to his family and neighbors the amazing instrument he had brought back from Lemberg. The word spread quickly and soon the people of Chelm were divided; some believed in the trumpet's powers and others maintained that Shlemiel had again been swindled. The matter would most certainly have come before the Elders, but it was summertime and they were not in session.

Shlemiel's father-in-law was one of those with no faith in the trumpet. "It's another billy goat," he said. Shlemiel was so eager to demonstrate what the trumpet could do that he decided to set his father-in-law's house on fire, intending, of course, to blow out the fire with the trumpet before any real damage was done.

His father-in-law's house was old and dry and it was soon enveloped in flames. Shlemiel blew his trumpet until he could blow no more, but, alas, the house continued to burn. The family was able to escape, but all their possessions were lost.

Despite the season, an emergency session of the Elders was called immediately. The Elders pondered the event for seven days and seven nights and came to the conclusion that a trumpet able to extinguish fires in Lemberg lost its power, for some unknown reason, in Chelm. Gronam the Ox proposed a law prohibiting the import of fire-fighting trumpets from Lemberg to Chelm. It was unanimously passed and duly recorded by Feyvel Thickwit.

Shlemiel had lost his wife's dowry and had burned down his father-in-law's house; nevertheless, he refused to give up the idea of going into business. Having failed in

Lublin and Lemberg, Shlemiel decided to do business with some local product in Chelm itself.

Chelm produced a sweet brandy that was Shlemiel's favorite drink. He decided to buy a keg of it and sell it in the market for three groschen a glass. He had figured out that if he could sell the whole kegful each day, he would make three-gulden profit a day. This time Mrs. Shlemiel made up her mind to help her husband. Shlemiel had no money left to pay the vintner, but his wife pawned a pin and they bought the brandy.

The following day they set up a small stand in the marketplace, placed the keg and a few glasses on it, and began hawking their drink to passers-by: "Sweet brandy, a refreshing and invigorating drink for all, three groschen a glass."

Sweet brandy was a popular drink in Chelm, but three groschen a glass was too high a price. Only one customer bought a glass, quite early in the day, and he paid for it with a three-groschen coin. When an hour had passed and there were no more buyers, Shlemiel began to lose heart. He became so restless that he needed a drink. He held the three-groschen coin in his hand and said to his wife: "In what way is my money inferior to another man's? Here is three groschen and sell me a drink."

Mrs. Shlemiel thought the matter over and said: "You are right, Shlemiel. Your coin is as good as anyone else's."

And she gave him a glass of brandy. Shlemiel drank it up and licked his lips. Most delicious! After a while Mrs. Shlemiel got thirsty too. And she said to Shlemiel: "In what way is my three-groschen piece worse than another's? Here is my money and let me have a drink."

To make a long story short, Shlemiel and Mrs. Shlemiel continued drinking and passing the coin between them all day long. When evening came, the best part of the keg's contents was consumed and all they had to show for the day's work was a single three-groschen coin.

Shlemiel and his wife tried in vain to figure out where they had made a mistake this time; no matter how they puzzled over the problem, they could not find the solution. They had sold almost an entire keg of sweet brandy for cash, but the cash was not to be seen. Shlemiel believed that not even the Elders of Chelm could explain what had happened to the money he and his wife had paid to each other.

This ended Shlemiel's attempts to go into business, and it was from that time on that Mrs. Shlemiel began to sell vegetables in the market. As for Shlemiel, he stayed at home and when the children were born took care of them. He also fed the chickens Mrs. Shlemiel kept under the stove.

Shlemiel's father-in-law was so disgusted with his son-in-law that he moved to Lublin. It was the first time in

the history of Chelm that one of its citizens left the village for good. Nevertheless, Mrs. Shlemiel, though she chided him, continued to admire her husband. Shlemiel would often say to her: "If the Lublin nanny goat had not turned into a billy goat, and if the trumpet had been able to extinguish fires in Chelm, I would now be the richest man in town."

To which Mrs. Shlemiel would reply: "You may be poor, Shlemiel, but you are certainly wise. Wisdom such as yours is rare even in Chelm."

Utzel &
His Daughter Poverty

Once there was a man named Utzel. He was very poor and even more lazy. Whenever anyone wanted to give him a job to do, his answer was always the same: "Not today."

"Why not today?" he was asked. And he always replied, "Why not tomorrow?"

Utzel lived in a cottage that had been built by his great-grandfather. The thatched roof needed mending and although the holes let the rain in, they did not let the smoke from the stove out. Toadstools grew on the crooked walls and the floor had rotted away. There had been a time when mice lived there, but now there weren't any because there was nothing for them to eat. Utzel's wife had starved to death, but before she died she had given birth to a baby girl. The name Utzel gave his daughter was very fitting. He called her Poverty.

Utzel loved to sleep and each night he went to bed with the chickens. In the morning he would complain that he was tired from so much sleeping and so he went to sleep again. When he was not sleeping, he lay on his broken-down cot, yawning and complaining. He would say to his daughter: "Other people are lucky. They have money without working. I am cursed."

Utzel was a small man, but as his daughter Poverty grew, she spread out in all directions. She was tall, broad, and heavy. At fifteen she had to lower her head to get through the doorway. Her feet were the size of a man's and puffy with fat. The villagers maintained that the lazier Utzel got, the more Poverty grew.

Utzel loved nobody, was jealous of everybody. He even spoke with envy of cats, dogs, rabbits, and all creatures who didn't have to work for a living. Yes, Utzel hated everybody and everything, but he adored his daughter. He daydreamed that a rich young man would fall in love with her, marry her, and provide for his wife and his father-in-law. But not a young man in the village showed the slightest interest in Poverty. When her father reproached the girl for not making friends and not going out with young men, Poverty would say: "How can I go out in rags and bare feet?"

One day Utzel learned that a certain charitable society in the village loaned poor people money, which they could pay back in small sums over a long period. Lazy as he was, he made a great effort—got up, dressed, and went to the office of the society. "I would like to borrow five gulden," he said to the official in charge.

"What do you intend to do with the money?" he was asked. "We only lend money for useful purposes."

"I want to have a pair of shoes made for my daughter," Utzel explained. "If Poverty has shoes, she will go out with the young people of the village and some wealthy young man will surely fall in love with her. When they get married, I will be able to pay back the five gulden."

The official thought it over. The chances of anyone falling in love with Poverty were very small. Utzel, however, looked so miserable that the official decided to give him the loan. He asked Utzel to sign a promissory note and gave him five gulden.

Utzel had tried to order a pair of shoes for his daughter a few months before. Sandler, the shoemaker, had gone so far as to take Poverty's measurements, but the shoemaker had wanted his money in advance. From the charitable society Utzel went directly to the shoemaker and asked him whether he still had Poverty's measurements.

"And supposing I do?" Sandler replied. "My price is five gulden and I still want my money in advance."

Utzel took out the five gulden and handed them to Sandler. The shoemaker opened a drawer and after some searching brought out the order for Poverty's shoes. He promised to deliver the new shoes in a week, on Friday.

Utzel, who wanted to surprise his daughter, did not tell her about the shoes. The following Friday, as he lay on his cot yawning and complaining, there was a knock on the door and Sandler came in carrying the new shoes. When Poverty saw the shoemaker with a pair of shiny, new shoes in his hand, she cried out in joy. The shoemaker handed her the shoes and told her to try them on. But, alas, she could not get them on her puffy feet. In the months since the measurements had been taken, Poverty's feet had become even larger than they were before. Now the girl cried out in grief.

Utzel looked on in consternation. "How is it possible?" he asked. "I thought her feet stopped growing long ago."

For a while Sandler, too, stood there puzzled. Then he inquired: "Tell me, Utzel, where did you get the five gulden?" Utzel explained that he had borrowed the money from the charitable loan society and had given them a promissory note in return.

"So now you have a debt," exclaimed Sandler. "That makes you even poorer than you were a few months ago. Then you had nothing, but today you have five gulden less than nothing. And since you have grown poorer, Poverty has grown bigger and naturally her feet have grown with her. That is why the shoes don't fit. It is all clear to me now."

"What are we going to do?" Utzel asked in despair.

"There is only one way out for you," Sandler said. "Go to work. From borrowing one gets poorer and from work one gets richer. When you and your daughter work, she will have shoes that fit."

The idea of working did not appeal to either of them, but it was even worse to have new shoes and go around barefoot. Utzel and Poverty both decided that immediately after the Sabbath they would look for work.

Utzel got a job as a water carrier. Poverty became a maid. For the first time in their lives, they worked diligently. They were kept so busy that they did not even think of the new shoes until one Sabbath morning Poverty decided she'd try them on again. Lo and behold, her feet slipped easily into them. The new shoes fit.

At last Utzel and Poverty understood that all a man possesses he gains through work, and not by lying in bed and being idle. Even animals are industrious. Bees make honey, spiders spin webs, birds build nests, moles dig holes in the earth, squirrels store food for the winter. Before long Utzel got a better job. He rebuilt his house and bought some furniture. Poverty lost more weight. She had new clothes made and dressed prettily like the other girls of the village. Her looks improved too, and a young man began to court her. His name was Mahir and he was the son of a wealthy merchant. Utzel's dream of a rich son-in-law came true, but by then he no longer needed to be taken care of.

Love for his daughter had saved Utzel. In his later years he became so respected he was elected a warden of that same charitable loan society from which he had borrowed five gulden.

On the wall of his office there hung the string with which Sandler had once measured Poverty's feet, and above it the framed motto: "Whatever you can do today, don't put off till tomorrow."

Menaseh's Dream

Menaseh was an orphan. He lived with his uncle Mendel, who was a poor glazier and couldn't even manage to feed and clothe his own children. Menaseh had already completed his cheder studies and after the fall holidays was to be apprenticed to a bookbinder.

Menaseh had always been a curious child. He had begun to ask questions as soon as he could talk: "How high is the sky?" "How deep is the earth?" "What is beyond the edge of the world?" "Why are people born?" "Why do they die?"

It was a hot and humid summer day. A golden haze hovered over the village. The sun was as small as a moon and yellow as brass. Dogs loped along with their tails between their legs. Pigeons rested in the middle of the marketplace. Goats sheltered themselves beneath the eaves of the huts, chewing their cuds and shaking their beards.

Menaseh quarreled with his aunt Dvosha and left the house without eating lunch. He was about twelve, with a longish face, black eyes, sunken cheeks. He wore a torn jacket and was barefoot. His only possession was a tattered storybook which he had read scores of times. It was called *Alone in the Wild Forest.* The village in which he lived stood in a forest that surrounded it like a sash and was said to stretch as far as Lublin. It was blueberry time and here and there one might also find wild strawberries. Menaseh made his way through pastures and wheat fields. He was hungry and he tore off a stalk of wheat to chew on the grain. In the meadows, cows were lying down, too hot even to whisk off the flies with their tails. Two horses stood, the head of one near the rump of the other, lost in their horse thoughts. In a field planted in buckwheat the boy was amazed to see a crow perched on the torn hat of a scarecrow.

Once Menaseh entered the forest, it was cooler. The pine trees stood straight as pillars and on their brownish bark hung golden necklaces, the light of the sun shining through the pine needles. The sounds of cuckoo and wood-pecker were heard, and an unseen bird kept repeating the same eerie screech.

Menaseh stepped carefully over moss pillows. He crossed a shallow streamlet that purled joyfully over pebbles and stones. The forest was still, and yet full of voices and echoes.

He wandered deeper and deeper into the forest. As a rule, he left stone markers behind, but not today. He was lonely, his head ached and his knees felt weak. "Am I get-ting sick?" he thought. "Maybe I'm going to die. Then I will soon be with Daddy and Mama." When he came to a blueberry patch, he sat down, picked one berry after another and popped them into his mouth. But they did not satisfy his hunger. Flowers with intoxicating odors grew among the blueberries. Without realizing it, Mena-seh stretched full length on the forest floor. He fell asleep, but in his dream he continued walking.

The trees became even taller, the smells stronger, huge birds flew from branch to branch. The sun was setting. The forest grew thinner and he soon came out on a plain with a broad view of the evening sky. Suddenly a castle appeared in the twilight. Menaseh had never seen such a beautiful structure. Its roof was of silver and from it rose a crystal tower. Its many tall windows were as high as the building itself. Menaseh went up to one of the windows and looked in. On the wall opposite him, he saw his own portrait hanging. He was dressed in luxurious clothes such as he had never owned. The huge room was empty.

"Why is the castle empty?" he wondered. "And why is my portrait hanging on the wall?" The boy in the picture seemed to be alive and waiting impatiently for someone to come. Then doors opened where there had been none before, and men and women came into the room. They were dressed in white satin and the women wore jewels and held holiday prayer books with gold-embossed covers. Menaseh gazed in astonishment. He recognized his father, his mother, his grandfathers and grandmothers, and other relatives. He wanted to rush over to them, hug and kiss them, but the window glass stood in his way. He began to cry. His paternal grandfather, Tobias the Scribe, separated himself from the group and came to the window. The old man's beard was as white as his long coat. He looked both ancient and young. "Why are you crying?" he asked. Despite the glass that separated them, Menaseh heard him clearly.

"Are you my grandfather Tobias?"

"Yes, my child. I am your grandfather."

"Who does this castle belong to?"

"To all of us."

"To me too?"

"Of course, to the whole family."

"Grandpa, let me in," Menaseh called. "I want to speak to my father and mother."

His grandfather looked at him lovingly and said: "One day you will live with us here, but the time has not yet come."

"How long do I have to wait?"

"That is a secret. It will not be for many, many years."

"Grandpa, I don't want to wait so long. I'm hungry and thirsty and tired. Please let me in. I miss my father and mother and you and Grandma. I don't want to be an orphan."

"My dear child. We know everything. We think about you and we love you. We are all waiting for the time when we will be together, but you must be patient. You have a long journey to take before you come here to stay."

"Please, just let me in for a few minutes."

Grandfather Tobias left the window and took counsel with other members of the family. When he returned, he said: "You may come in, but only for a little while. We will show you around the castle and let you see some of our treasures, but then you must leave."

A door opened and Menaseh stepped inside. He was no sooner over the threshold than his hunger and weariness left him. He embraced his parents and they kissed and hugged him. But they didn't utter a word. He felt strangely light. He floated along and his family floated with him. His grandfather opened door after door and each time Menaseh's astonishment grew.

One room was filled with racks of boys' clothing—pants, jackets, shirts, coats. Menaseh realized that these were the clothes he had worn as far back as he could remember. He also recognized his shoes, socks, caps, and nightshirts.

A second door opened and he saw all the toys he had ever owned: the tin soldiers his father had bought him; the jumping clown his mother had brought back from the fair at Lublin; the whistles and harmonicas; the teddy bear Grandfather had given him one Purim and the wooden horse that was the gift of Grandmother Sprintze on his sixth birthday. The notebooks in which he had practiced writing, his pencils and Bible lay on a table. The Bible was open at the title page, with its familiar engraving of Moses holding the holy tablets and Aaron in his priestly robes, both framed by a border of six-winged angels. He noticed his name in the space allowed for it.

Menaseh could hardly overcome his wonder when a third door opened. This room was filled with soap bubbles. They did not burst as soap bubbles do, but floated serenely about, reflecting all the colors of the rainbow.

Some of them mirrored castles, gardens, rivers, windmills, and many other sights. Menaseh knew that these were the bubbles he used to blow from his favorite bubble pipe. Now they seemed to have a life of their own.

A fourth door opened. Menaseh entered a room with no one in it, yet it was full of the sounds of happy talk, song, and laughter. Menaseh heard his own voice and the songs he used to sing when he lived at home with his parents. He also heard the voices of his former playmates, some of whom he had long since forgotten.

The fifth door led to a large hall. It was filled with the characters in the stories his parents had told him at bedtime and with the heroes and heroines of *Alone in the Wild Forest*. They were all there: David the Warrior and the Ethiopian princess, whom David saved from captivity; the highwayman Bandurek, who robbed the rich and fed the poor; Velikan the giant, who had one eye in the center of his forehead and who carried a fir tree as a staff in his right hand and a snake in his left; the midget Pitzeles, whose beard dragged on the ground and who was jester to the fearsome King Merodach; and the two-headed wizard Malkizedek, who by witchcraft spirited innocent girls into the desert of Sodom and Gomorrah.

Menaseh barely had time to take them all in when a sixth door opened. Here everything was changing constantly. The walls of the room turned like a carousel.

Events flashed by. A golden horse became a blue butter-fly; a rose as bright as the sun became a goblet out of which flew fiery grasshoppers, purple fauns, and silver bats. On a glittering throne with seven steps leading up to it sat King Solomon, who somehow resembled Menaseh. He wore a crown and at his feet knelt the Queen of Sheba. A peacock spread his tail and addressed King Solomon in Hebrew. The priestly Levites played their lyres. Giants waved their swords in the air and Ethiopian slaves riding lions served goblets of wine and trays filled with pome-granates. For a moment Menaseh did not understand what it all meant. Then he realized that he was seeing his dreams.

Behind the seventh door, Menaseh glimpsed men and women, animals, and many things that were completely strange to him. The images were not as vivid as they had been in the other rooms. The figures were transparent and surrounded by mist. On the threshold there stood a girl Menaseh's own age. She had long golden braids. Although Menaseh could not see her clearly, he liked her at once. For the first time he turned to his grandfather. "What is all this?" he asked. And his grandfather replied: "These are the people and events of your future."

"Where am I?" Menaseh asked.

"You are in a castle that has many names. We like to call it the place where nothing is lost. There are many

more wonders here, but now it is time for you to leave."

Menaseh wanted to remain in this strange place forever, together with his parents and grandparents. He looked questioningly at his grandfather, who shook his head. Menaseh's parents seemed to want him both to remain and to leave as quickly as possible. They still did not speak, but signaled to him, and Menaseh understood that he was in grave danger. This must be a forbidden place. His parents silently bade him farewell and his face became wet and hot from their kisses. At that moment everything disappeared—the castle, his parents, his grandparents, the girl.

Menaseh shivered and awoke. It was night in the forest. Dew was falling. High above the crowns of the pine trees, the full moon shone and the stars twinkled. Menaseh looked into the face of a girl who was bending over him. She was barefoot and wore a patched skirt; her long braided hair shone golden in the moonlight. She was shaking him and saying: "Get up, get up. It is late and you can't remain here in the forest."

Menaseh sat up. "Who are you?"

"I was looking for berries and I found you here. I've been trying to wake you."

"What is your name?"

"Channeleh. We moved into the village last week."

She looked familiar, but he could not remember meeting

her before. Suddenly he knew. She was the girl he had seen in the seventh room, before he woke up.

"You lay there like dead. I was frightened when I saw you. Were you dreaming? Your face was so pale and your lips were moving."

"Yes, I did have a dream."

"What about?"

"A castle."

"What kind of castle?"

Menaseh did not reply and the girl did not repeat her question. She stretched out her hand to him and helped him get up. Together they started toward home. The moon had never seemed so light or the stars so close. They walked with their shadows behind them. Myriads of crickets chirped. Frogs croaked with human voices.

Menaseh knew that his uncle would be angry at him for coming home late. His aunt would scold him for leaving without his lunch. But these things no longer mattered. In his dream he had visited a mysterious world. He had found a friend. Channeleh and he had already decided to go berry picking the next day.

Among the undergrowth and wild mushrooms, little people in red jackets, gold caps, and green boots emerged. They danced in a circle and sang a song which is heard only by those who know that everything lives and nothing in time is ever lost.

When Shlemiel Went
to Warsaw

Though Shlemiel was a lazybones and a sleepyhead and hated to move, he always daydreamed of taking a trip. He had heard many stories about faraway countries, huge deserts, deep oceans, and high mountains, and often discussed with Mrs. Shlemiel his great wish to go on a long journey. Mrs. Shlemiel would reply: "Long journeys are not for a Shlemiel. You better stay home and mind the children while I go to market to sell my vegetables." Yet Shlemiel could not bring himself to give up his dream of seeing the world and its wonders.

A recent visitor to Chelm had told Shlemiel marvelous things about the city of Warsaw. How beautiful the streets were, how high the buildings and luxurious the stores. Shlemiel decided once and for all that he must see this great city for himself. He knew that one had to prepare for a journey. But what was there for him to take? He had nothing but the old clothes he wore. One morning, after Mrs. Shlemiel left for the market, he told the older boys to stay home from cheder and mind the younger children. Then he took a few slices of bread, an onion, and a clove of garlic, put them in a kerchief, tied it into a bundle, and started for Warsaw on foot.

There was a street in Chelm called Warsaw Street and Shlemiel believed that it led directly to Warsaw. While still in the village, he was stopped by several neighbors who asked him where he was going. Shlemiel told them that he was on his way to Warsaw.

"What will you do in Warsaw?" they asked him.

Shlemiel replied: "What do I do in Chelm? Nothing."

He soon reached the outskirts of town. He walked slowly because the soles of his boots were worn through. Soon the houses and stores gave way to pastures and fields. He passed a peasant driving an ox-drawn plow. After several hours of walking, Shlemiel grew tired. He was so weary that he wasn't even hungry. He lay down on the grass near the roadside for a nap, but before he

fell asleep he thought: "When I wake up, I may not remember which is the way to Warsaw and which leads
back to Chelm." After pondering a moment, he removed
his boots and set them down beside him with the toes
pointing toward Warsaw and the heels toward Chelm. He
soon fell asleep and dreamed that he was a baker baking
onion rolls with poppy seeds. Customers came to buy them
and Shlemiel said: "These onion rolls are not for sale."

"Then why do you bake them?"

"They are for my wife, my children, and for me."

Later he dreamed that he was the king of Chelm. Once
a year, instead of taxes, each citizen brought him a pot
of strawberry jam. Shlemiel sat on a golden throne and
nearby sat Mrs. Shlemiel, the queen, and his children, the
princes and princesses. They were all eating onion rolls
and spooning up big portions of strawberry jam. A carriage
arrived and took the royal family to Warsaw, America,
and to the River Sambation, which spurts out stones the
week long and rests on the Sabbath.

Near the road, a short distance from where Shlemiel
slept, was a smithy. The blacksmith happened to come
out just in time to see Shlemiel carefully placing his boots
at his side with the toes facing in the direction of Warsaw. The blacksmith was a prankster and as soon as
Shlemiel was sound asleep he tiptoed over and turned the
boots around. When Shlemiel awoke, he felt rested but

hungry. He got out a slice of bread, rubbed it with garlic, and took a bite of onion. Then he pulled his boots on and continued on his way.

He walked along and everything looked strangely familiar. He recognized houses that he had seen before. It seemed to him that he knew the people he met. Could it be that he had already reached another town, Shlemiel wondered. And why was it so similar to Chelm? He stopped a passer-by and asked the name of the town. "Chelm," the man replied.

Shlemiel was astonished. How was this possible? He had walked away from Chelm. How could he have arrived back there? He began to rub his forehead and soon found the answer to the riddle. There were two Chelms and he had reached the second one.

Still it seemed very odd that the streets, the houses, the people were so similar to those in the Chelm he had left behind. Shlemiel puzzled over this fact until he suddenly remembered something he had learned in cheder: "The earth is the same everywhere." And so why shouldn't the second Chelm be exactly like the first one? This discovery gave Shlemiel great satisfaction. He wondered if there was a street here like his street and a house on it like the one he lived in. And indeed he soon arrived at an identical street and house. Evening had fallen. He opened the door and to his amazement saw a second Mrs. Shlemiel

with children just like his. Everything was exactly the same as in his own household. Even the cat seemed the same. Mrs. Shlemiel at once began to scold him.

"Shlemiel, where did you go? You left the house alone. And what have you there in that bundle?"

The children all ran to him and cried: "Papa, where have you been?"

Shlemiel paused a moment and then he said: "Mrs. Shlemiel, I'm not your husband. Children, I'm not your papa."

"Have you lost your mind?" Mrs. Shlemiel screamed.

"I am Shlemiel of Chelm One and this is Chelm Two."

Mrs. Shlemiel clapped her hands so hard that the chickens sleeping under the stove awoke in fright and flew out all over the room.

"Children, your father has gone crazy," she wailed. She immediately sent one of the boys for Gimpel, the healer. All the neighbors came crowding in. Shlemiel stood in the middle of the room and proclaimed: "It's true, you all look like the people in my town, but you are not the same. I come from Chelm One and you live in Chelm Two."

"Shlemiel, what's the matter with you?" someone cried. "You're in your own house, with your own wife and children, your own neighbors and friends."

"No, you don't understand. I come from Chelm One.

I was on my way to Warsaw, and between Chelm One and Warsaw there is a Chelm Two. And that is where I am."

"What are you talking about. We all know you and you know all of us. Don't you recognize your chickens?"

"No, I'm not in my town," Shlemiel insisted. "But," he continued, "Chelm Two does have the same people and the same houses as Chelm One, and that is why you are mistaken. Tomorrow I will continue on to Warsaw."

"In that case, where is my husband?" Mrs. Shlemiel inquired in a rage, and she proceeded to berate Shlemiel with all the curses she could think of.

"How should I know where your husband is?" Shlemiel replied.

Some of the neighbors could not help laughing; others pitied the family. Gimpel, the healer, announced that he knew of no remedy for such an illness. After some time, everybody went home.

Mrs. Shlemiel had cooked noodles and beans that evening, a dish that Shlemiel liked especially. She said to him: "You may be mad, but even a madman has to eat."

"Why should you feed a stranger?" Shlemiel asked.

"As a matter of fact, an ox like you should eat straw, not noodles and beans. Sit down and be quiet. Maybe some food and rest will bring you back to your senses."

"Mrs. Shlemiel, you're a good woman. My wife wouldn't

feed a stranger. It would seem that there is some small difference between the two Chelms."

The noodles and beans smelled so good that Shlemiel needed no further coaxing. He sat down and as he ate he spoke to the children.

"My dear children, I live in a house that looks exactly like this one. I have a wife and she is as like your mother as two peas are like each other. My children resemble you as drops of water resemble one another."

The younger children laughed; the older ones began to cry. Mrs. Shlemiel said: "As if being a Shlemiel wasn't enough, he had to go crazy in addition. What am I going to do now? I won't be able to leave the children with him when I go to market. Who knows what a madman may do?" She clasped her head in her hands and cried out: "God in heaven, what have I done to deserve this?"

Nevertheless, she made up a fresh bed for Shlemiel; and even though he had napped during the day, near the smithy, the moment his head touched the pillow he fell fast asleep and was soon snoring loudly. He again dreamed that he was the king of Chelm and that his wife, the queen, had fried for him a huge panful of blintzes. Some were filled with cheese, others with blueberries or cherries, and all were sprinkled with sugar and cinnamon and were drowning in sour cream. Shlemiel ate twenty blintzes all at once and hid the remainder in his crown for later.

In the morning, when Shlemiel awoke, the house was filled with townspeople. Mrs. Shlemiel stood in their midst, her eyes red with weeping. Shlemiel was about to scold his wife for letting so many strangers into the house, but then he remembered that he himself was a stranger here. At home he would have gotten up, washed, and dressed. Now in front of all these people he was at a loss as to what to do. As always when he was embarrassed, he began to scratch his head and pull at his beard. Finally, overcoming his bashfulness, he decided to get up. He threw off the covers and put his bare feet on the floor. "Don't let him run away," Mrs. Shlemiel screamed. "He'll disappear and I'll be a deserted wife, without a Shlemiel."

At this point Baruch, the baker, interrupted. "Let's take him to the Elders. They'll know what to do."

"That's right! Let's take him to the Elders," everybody agreed.

Although Shlemiel insisted that since he lived in Chelm One, the local Elders had no power over him, several of the strong young men helped him into his pants, his boots, his coat and cap and escorted him to the house of Gronam the Ox. The Elders, who had already heard of the matter, had gathered early in the morning to consider what was to be done.

As the crowd came in, one of the Elders, Dopey Lekisch, was saying, "Maybe there really are two Chelms."

"If there are two, then why can't there be three, four, or even a hundred Chelms?" Sender Donkey interrupted.

"And even if there are a hundred Chelms, must there be a Shlemiel in each one of them?" argued Shmendrick Numskull.

Gronam the Ox, the head Elder, listened to all the arguments but was not yet prepared to express an opinion. However, his wrinkled, bulging forehead indicated that he was deep in thought. It was Gronam the Ox who questioned Shlemiel. Shlemiel related everything that had happened to him, and when he finished, Gronam asked: "Do you recognize me?"

"Surely. You are wise Gronam the Ox."

"And in your Chelm is there also a Gronam the Ox?"

"Yes, there is a Gronam the Ox and he looks exactly like you."

"Isn't it possible that you turned around and came back to Chelm?" Gronam inquired.

"Why should I turn around? I'm not a windmill," Shlemiel replied.

"In that case, you are not this Mrs. Shlemiel's husband."

"No, I'm not."

"Then Mrs. Shlemiel's husband, the real Shlemiel, must have left the day you came."

"It would seem so."

"Then he'll probably come back."

"Probably."

"In that case, you must wait until he returns. Then we'll know who is who."

"Dear Elders, my Shlemiel has come back," screamed Mrs. Shlemiel. "I don't need two Shlemiels. One is more than enough."

"Whoever he is, he may not live in your house until everything is made clear," Gronam insisted.

"Where shall I live?" Shlemiel asked.

"In the poorhouse."

"What will I do in the poorhouse?"

"What do you do at home?"

"Good God, who will take care of my children when I go to market?" moaned Mrs. Shlemiel. "Besides, I want a husband. Even a Shlemiel is better than no husband at all."

"Are we to blame that your husband left you and went to Warsaw?" Gronam asked. "Wait until he comes home."

Mrs. Shlemiel wept bitterly and the children cried too. Shlemiel said: "How strange. My own wife always scolded me. My children talked back to me. And here a strange woman and strange children want me to live with them. It looks to me as if Chelm Two is actually better than Chelm One."

"Just a moment. I think I have an idea," interrupted Gronam.

"What is your idea?" Zeinvel Ninny inquired.

"Since we decided to send Shlemiel to the poorhouse, the town will have to hire someone to take care of Mrs. Shlemiel's children so she can go to market. Why not hire Shlemiel for that? It's true, he is not Mrs. Shlemiel's husband or the children's father. But he is so much like the real Shlemiel that the children will feel at home with him."

"What a wonderful idea!" cried Feyvel Thickwit.

"Only King Solomon could have thought of such a wise solution," agreed Treitel the Fool.

"Such a clever way out of this dilemma could only have been thought of in our Chelm," chimed in Shmendrick Numskull.

"How much do you want to be paid to take care of Mrs. Shlemiel's children?" asked Gronam.

For a moment Shlemiel stood there completely bewildered. Then he said, "Three groschen a day."

"Idiot, moron, ass!" screamed Mrs. Shlemiel. "What are three groschen nowadays? You shouldn't do it for less than six a day." She ran over to Shlemiel and pinched him on the arm. Shlemiel winced and cried out, "She pinches just like my wife."

The Elders held a consultation among themselves. The

town budget was very limited. Finally Gronam announced: "Three groschen may be too little, but six groschen a day is definitely too much, especially for a stranger. We will compromise and pay you five groschen a day. Shlemiel, do you accept?"

"Yes, but how long am I to keep this job?"

"Until the real Shlemiel comes home."

Gronam's decision was soon known throughout Chelm and the town admired his great wisdom and that of all the Elders of Chelm.

At first, Shlemiel tried to keep for himself the five groschen that the town paid him. "If I'm not your husband, I don't have to support you," he told Mrs. Shlemiel.

"In that case, since I'm not your wife, I don't have to cook for you, darn your socks, or patch your clothes."

And so, of course, Shlemiel turned over his pay to her. It was the first time that Mrs. Shlemiel had ever gotten any money for the household from Shlemiel. Now when she was in a good mood, she would say to him: "What a pity you didn't decide to go to Warsaw ten years ago."

"Don't you ever miss your husband?" Shlemiel would ask.

"And what about you? Don't you miss your wife?" Mrs. Shlemiel would ask.

And both would admit that they were quite happy with matters as they stood.

Years passed and no Shlemiel returned to Chelm. The Elders had many explanations for this. Zeinvel Ninny believed that Shlemiel had crossed the black mountains and had been eaten alive by the cannibals who live there. Dopey Lekisch thought that Shlemiel most probably had come to the Castle of Asmodeus, where he had been forced to marry a demon princess. Shmendrick Numskull came to the conclusion that Shlemiel had reached the edge of the world and had fallen off. There were many other theories. For example, that the real Shlemiel had lost his memory and had simply forgotten that he was Shlemiel. Such things do happen.

Gronam did not like to impose his theories on other people; however, he was convinced that Shlemiel had gone to the other Chelm, where he had had exactly the same experience as the Shlemiel in this Chelm. He had been hired by the local community and was taking care of the other Mrs. Shlemiel's children for a wage of five groschen a day.

As for Shlemiel himself, he no longer knew what to think. The children were growing up and soon would be able to take care of themselves. Sometimes Shlemiel would sit and ponder. Where is the other Shlemiel? When will he come home? What is my real wife doing? Is she waiting for me, or has she got herself another Shlemiel? These were questions that he could not answer.

Every now and then Shlemiel would still get the desire to go traveling, but he could not bring himself to start out. What was the point of going on a trip if it led nowhere? Often, as he sat alone puzzling over the strange ways of the world, he would become more and more confused and begin humming to himself:

> *"Those who leave Chelm*
> *End up in Chelm.*
> *Those who remain in Chelm*
> *Are certainly in Chelm.*
> *All roads lead to Chelm.*
> *All the world is one big Chelm."*